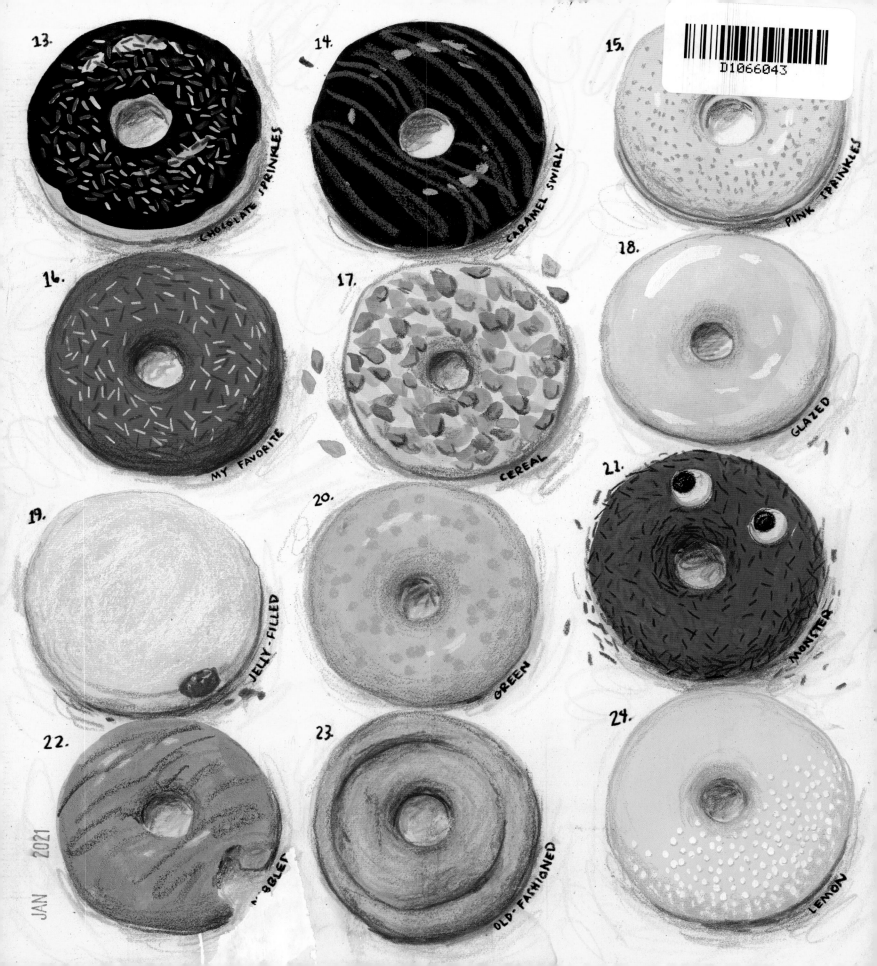

13.
CHOCOLATE SPRINKLES

14.
CARAMEL SWIRLY

15.
PINK SPRINKLES

16.
MY FAVORITE

17.
CEREAL

18.
GLAZED

19.
JELLY-FILLED

20.
GREEN

21.
MONSTER

22.
NIBBLED

23.
OLD-FASHIONED

24.
LEMON

JAN 2021

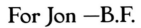

For Jay, Eben, and Mia—my favorite doughnut sharers,
and for my mother, for Fridays —C.F.

For Jon —B.F.

G. P. PUTNAM'S SONS
An imprint of Penguin Random House LLC, New York

Text copyright © 2020 by Carrie Finison
Illustrations copyright © 2020 by Brianne Farley
Penguin supports copyright. Copyright fuels creativity, encourages diverse voices, promotes free speech,
and creates a vibrant culture. Thank you for buying an authorized edition of this book and for complying with
copyright laws by not reproducing, scanning, or distributing any part of it in any form without permission.
You are supporting writers and allowing Penguin to continue to publish books for every reader.

G. P. Putnam's Sons is a registered trademark of Penguin Random House LLC.

Visit us online at penguinrandomhouse.com

Library of Congress Cataloging-in-Publication Data
Names: Finison, Carrie, author | Farley, Brianne, illustrator.
Title: Dozens of doughnuts / Carrie Finison; illustrated by Brianne Farley.
Description: New York: G. P. Putnam's Sons, [2020] | Summary: A generous but increasingly put-upon bear
makes batch after batch of doughnuts for her woodland friends without saving any for herself.
Identifiers: LCCN 2019020194 | ISBN 9780525518358 (hardcover) | ISBN 9780525518365 (epub fxl cpb) |
ISBN 9780525518372 (kf8/kindle)
Subjects: | CYAC: Sharing—Fiction. | Doughnuts—Fiction. | Baking—Fiction. | Bears—Fiction. | Forest animals—Fiction.
Classification: LCC PZ8.3.F623 Do 2020 | DDC [E]—dc23
LC record available at https://lccn.loc.gov/2019020194

Manufactured in China by RR Donnelley Asia Printing Solutions Ltd.
ISBN 9780525518358
1 3 5 7 9 10 8 6 4 2

Design by Marikka Tamura
Text set in P22 Parrish
The art was done in gouache, colored pencil, and charcoal,
with some help from Photoshop.

DOZENS OF DOUGHNUTS

written by
CARRIE FINISON

illustrated by
BRIANNE FARLEY

putnam

G. P. P   s Sons

"Sure," says LouAnn, and she pulls up a chair.

One dozen doughnuts, hot from the pan.
Half are for Woodrow, the rest for—

DING-DONG!

"Clyde?"

LouAnn, feeling generous,
offers her plateful.

"Doughnuts? My favorite!"
says Clyde. "I'm so grateful!"

"You're welcome. Dig in!
I'll make more," says LouAnn.

She measures and mixes
as fast as she can.

FLOUR

One dozen doughnuts, hot from the pan.
A few for her friends, and the rest for—

DING-DONG!

"Topsy?"

"I smelled something good. Can I hang for a while?"
LouAnn says, "Come in," but she's lost her big smile.

"Delicious!" cries Topsy.
She gulps down a swallow.

LouAnn's heart feels warm,
but her belly feels hollow.

One dozen doughnuts, hot from the pan.
Some for each friend, and the rest for—

"Mouffette?"

Mouffette is so shy that she hides in a shrub.
LouAnn heaves a sigh and says, "Come join the club."

While her guests eat the doughnuts,
LouAnn starts to worry.
She cracks her last egg
and pours milk in a hurry.

The last dozen doughnuts! Hot from the pan.
A pair for each friend means there's MORE for—

DING-♪
DONG!

"Chip and Chomp?"

"It sounds like a party!"
They both scamper in.

They fill up their cheeks.
"Now, let winter begin!"

Woodrow pours cider. They all raise a toast,
but LouAnn is FED UP with her job as their host.

She's ready to sleep through the snow, ice, and sleet.
But winter is near, and there's NOTHING to eat!

Deep in her throat, there's a low, hungry grumble.
It slowly grows louder. Her friends hear the rumble.

One look at LouAnn, and they dash for the door.
After all, she's a bear, and she's ready to

She fusses

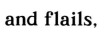and flails,

and then slowly grows still.

Snowflakes drift down. All is quiet, until—

DING-
DONG!
♪

Peeking outside, LouAnn blinks in surprise.
Her friends have come back, and they all brought supplies!

"We counted the doughnuts you made us. So many!
And that's when we noticed you didn't get ANY!"

WE'RE SORRY LOUANN!

Topsy ties aprons.

They prop LouAnn's feet.

Chip measures.
Chomp mixes.

Mouffette checks the heat.

Dozens of doughnuts, hot from the pan.
Stacked up in heaps, and they're ALL for LouAnn!

But her friends have made more than enough for one bear.
She has plenty to eat, and she's happy to share.

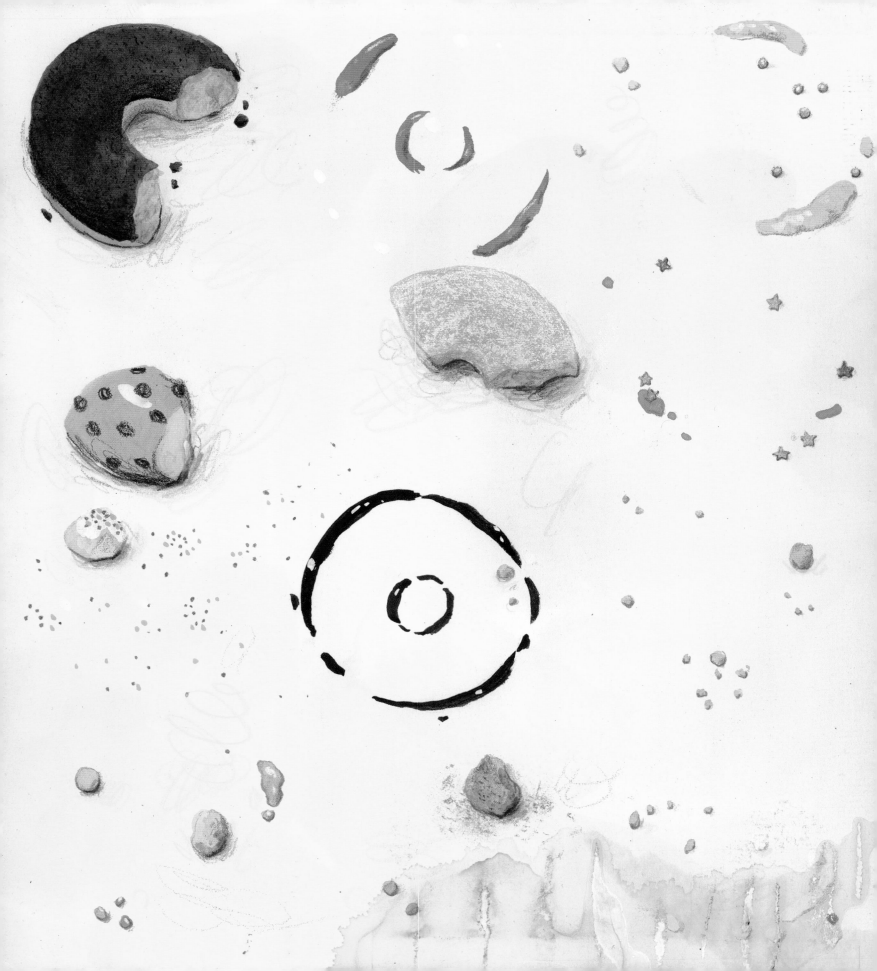